Kay Winters

This School Year Will Be THE BEST!

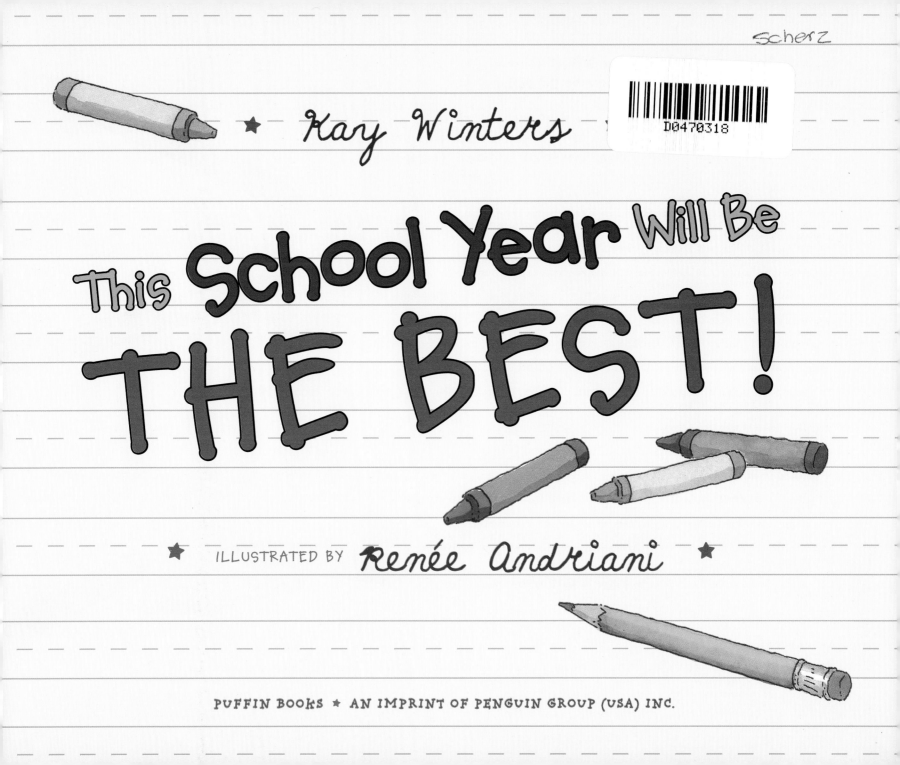

ILLUSTRATED BY **Renée Andriani**

PUFFIN BOOKS ★ AN IMPRINT OF PENGUIN GROUP (USA) INC.

To Linda Dicker, teacher, and Eileen Wessel, principal,
who know how to make each school year be the BEST!
—K.W.

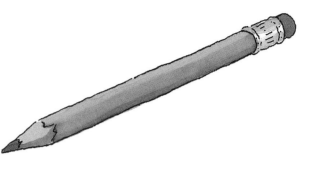

To the terrific teachers and students at Corinth
Elementary School in Prairie Village, Kansas
—R.A.

PUFFIN BOOKS
Published by the Penguin Group
Penguin Group (USA) Inc., 345 Hudson Street, New York, New York 10014, U.S.A.
Penguin Group (Canada), 90 Eglinton Avenue East, Suite 700, Toronto, Ontario M4P 2Y3, Canada
(a division of Pearson Penguin Canada Inc.)
Penguin Books Ltd, 80 Strand, London WC2R 0RL, England
Penguin Ireland, 25 St Stephen's Green, Dublin 2, Ireland (a division of Penguin Books Ltd)
Penguin Group (Australia), 707 Collins Street, Melbourne, Victoria 3008, Australia
(a division of Pearson Australia Group Pty Ltd)
Penguin Books India Pvt Ltd, 11 Community Centre, Panchsheel Park, New Delhi–110 017, India
Penguin Group (NZ), 67 Apollo Drive, Rosedale, Auckland 0632, New Zealand
(a division of Pearson New Zealand Ltd)
Penguin Books, Rosebank Office Park, 181 Jan Smuts Avenue, Parktown North 2193, South Africa
Penguin China, B7 Jiaming Center, 27 East Third Ring Road North, Chaoyang District, Beijing 100020, China

Penguin Books Ltd, Registered Offices: 80 Strand, London WC2R 0RL, England

First published in the United States of America by Dutton Children's Books, a division of Penguin Young Readers Group, 2010
Published by Puffin Books, an imprint of Penguin Young Readers Group, 2013

20 19 18 17 16 15 14 13

Text copyright © Kay Winters, 2010
Illustrations copyright © Renée Andriani, 2010
All rights reserved

THE LIBRARY OF CONGRESS HAS CATALOGED THE DUTTON CHILDREN'S BOOKS EDITION AS FOLLOWS:
Winters, Kay.
This school year will be the best! / Kay Winters ; illustrated by Renee Andriani.
Summary: When a teacher asks her students on the first day of school what they wish
for in the coming year, the answers range from having a good school picture to receiving
a perfect report card.
ISBN 978-0-525-42275-4 (hardcover)
[1. First day of school—Fiction. 2. Schools—Fiction.] I. Andriani, Renee, ill. II. Title.
PZ7.W7675 Th 2010   2009029394

Puffin Books 978-0-14-242696-8

Manufactured in the USA

Today was the first day of school.

We went to the rug and sat in a circle. Our teacher asked, "What do you hope will happen this year?"

We each shared a wish. I went first.

I hope I get the *best seat* on the bus.

This year I hope
I'll remember
my **homework**.

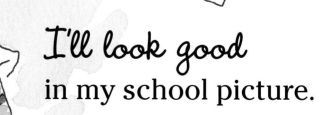

I'll look good
in my school picture.

We'll have a **chocolate fountain** at lunch!

This year
I'll kick the ball into
the right goal.

On the day the fire truck comes,
I'll be the one to **squirt the hose**.

We'll take **a field trip**
to someplace really cool.

I hope **I won't be a vegetable** in our school play!

I want to take the class pet home for winter break.

Our mom will bring a
BIRTHDAY SURPRISE to school.

I hope we get at least **one snow day**.

This year I'll **win the science fair**.

I hope I'll *make friends* in my new school.

When the nurse measures me,
I'll be tall.

I hope our *butterflies* will hatch.

We'll have **SKATEBOARD DAY**.

I won't **Lose things** in my desk.

The principal will
do something crazy!

My *report card*
will be perfect!

Then our teacher told us her wish.
I'll **get to know** each one of you.